This book is dedicated to our three sons,
Brian, John Thomas, and Trent. Parenthood
has been the joy of our lives and the
inspiration to love our students like they
were our own children.

-Mary Beth and Mike Young

BASEBALL ABCs

NATIONAL BASEBALL HALL OF FAME AND MUSEUM

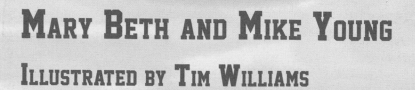

MARY BETH AND MIKE YOUNG

ILLUSTRATED BY TIM WILLIAMS

A is for Autumn Glory. Every autumn, the best teams in baseball play each other in the World Series. In the Baseball Hall of Fame, you can read about, hear, and watch some of the most exciting plays in World Series history.

B

is for Bullpen Theater. On the first floor of the Hall of Fame, you can experience many baseball videos, trivia games, and learn about baseball's greatest relief pitchers in the Bullpen Theater.

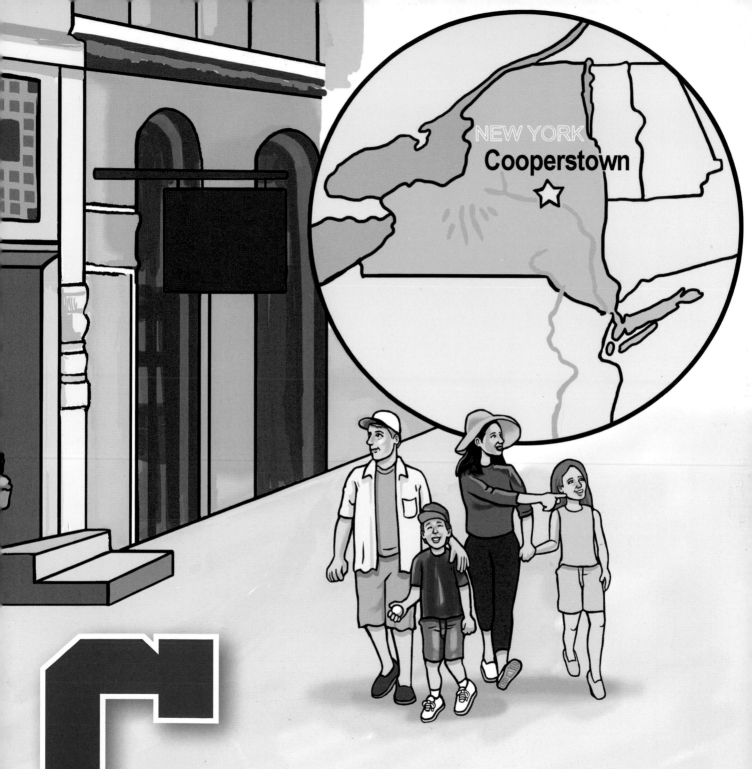

NEW YORK

Cooperstown

C

is for Cooperstown. Cooperstown is a small village in the state of New York that is world-famous as the home of the Baseball Hall of Fame.

D

is for Doubleday. Abner Doubleday is known as the inventor of the game of baseball. When you are in Cooperstown, walk down the street from the Hall of Fame and watch a game at Doubleday Field.

E

is for Experience. At the Hall of Fame's Baseball Experience, it feels like you are at a real game sitting in the grandstand cheering for your favorite players.

F is for Fans and Field of Dreams. For baseball fans, the Hall of Fame is a Field of Dreams.

G is for Giamatti Research Center. If you are a really big baseball fan, you can learn everything there is to know about the history of baseball in the Giamatti Research Center.

H is for Hank Aaron's Gallery of Records. Hank Aaron was one of the greatest home run hitters in baseball history. His 755 home run record is 2nd all-time and his chase of Babe Ruth's record was one of the most exciting baseball events ever.

I is for Inductees Row. At Inductees Row, you can see baseball artifacts from the newest members elected to the Hall of Fame. You can also view pictures of past Hall of Fame weekends.

J is for July. The new members elected to the Hall of Fame get inducted in July. This is the most exciting weekend of the year in Cooperstown.

K is for Kids. In the Sandlot Kids' Clubhouse on the first floor of the Hall of Fame, you can engage in the interactive displays, play games, and watch video clips.

L is for League of Their Own. Did you know that women have been important to the history of baseball? During World War II, a women's baseball league was formed that was made famous in the movie *A League of Their Own*.

M

is for Museum. The Baseball Hall of Fame is an example of a museum. Some museums have dinosaurs, some have paintings, but this one is dedicated to the wonderful game of baseball.

N

is for Negro Leagues. A long time ago, black players and white players were not allowed to play baseball together. The Hall of Fame has plenty of pictures and equipment from the days when black men played in a league by themselves.

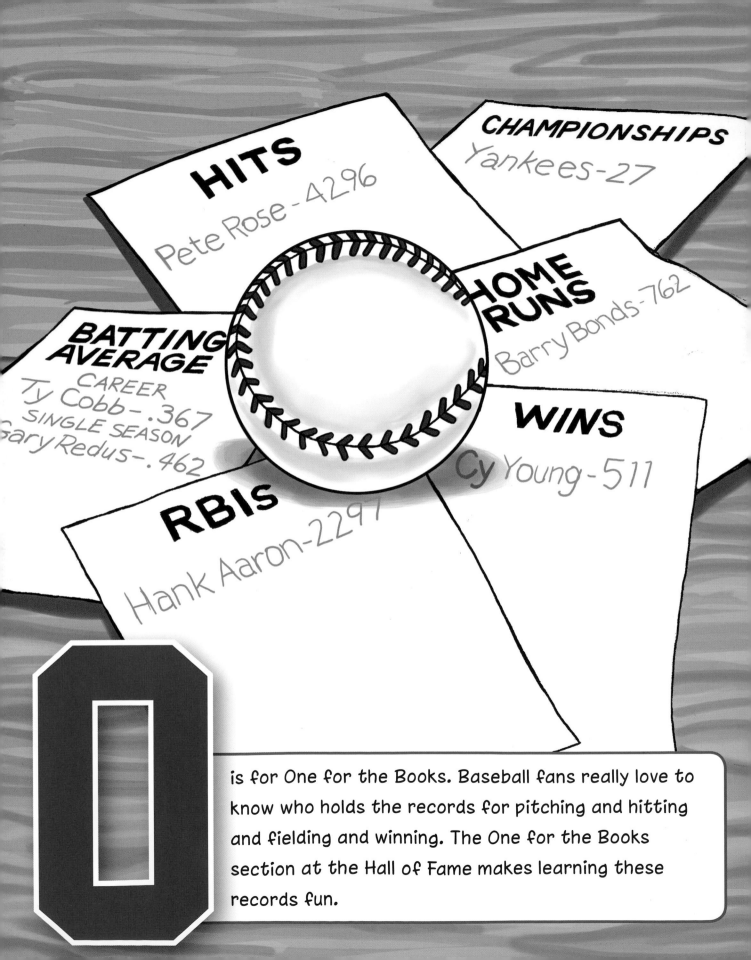

HITS
Pete Rose - 4296

CHAMPIONSHIPS
Yankees-27

HOME RUNS
Barry Bonds-762

BATTING AVERAGE
CAREER
Ty Cobb - .367
SINGLE SEASON
Gary Redus - .462

WINS
Cy Young-511

RBIs
Hank Aaron-2297

O

is for One for the Books. Baseball fans really love to know who holds the records for pitching and hitting and fielding and winning. The One for the Books section at the Hall of Fame makes learning these records fun.

CALVIN EDWIN RIPKEN JR.
"CAL" "IRON MAN"
BALTIMORE, A.L., 1981-2001

ARRIVED AT THE BALLPARK EVERY DAY WITH A BURNING DESIRE TO PERFORM AT HIS HIGHEST LEVEL. DEDICATION AND WORK ETHIC RESULTED IN A RECORD 2,632 CONSECUTIVE GAMES PLAYED FROM MAY 30, 1982 THROUGH SEPTEMBER 19, 1998. EARNING HIM THE TITLE OF BASEBALL'S "IRON MAN." IN 21 SEASONS, COLLECTED 3,184 HITS AND 431 HOME RUNS, AND WAS NAMED TO 19 CONSECUTIVE

P

is for Plaque Gallery. Every player, umpire, and manager enshrined in the Hall of Fame has a bronze plaque in the gallery telling you what they accomplished to become a member of baseball's most exclusive family.

is for Quiet. When you visit the Baseball at the Movies section, you don't have to be quiet like you do when you are at the theater. In this section, you can see memorable items from the great movies that have been made about baseball. There are over 250 movies, series, and documentaries made about baseball.

is for Ruth. Babe Ruth was one of baseball's first superstars. During his years with the New York Yankees, he became one of the most popular men in America.

S

is for Superior. The Hall of Fame cares about future Hall of Famers like you. The BASE program, Be A Superior Example, provides kids with healthy character building lifestyle choices.

Fruits
Grains
Veggies
Protein
Dairy

BASE PROGRAM

Be a Superior Example

Report Card
Math——A
English—A
Science-B
History—A
Attendance-A

T

is for Today. At the Today's Game exhibit, you can see what a real baseball locker room looks like for all thirty current major league teams. You can see jerseys, hats, bats, gloves, and cleats.

U is for Umpire. Umpires make sure the game of baseball is played fairly. They are so important that many umpires have been elected to the Hall of Fame, just like the game's greatest players.

Roberto Clemente
1973 Hall of Fame
inductee

V is for ¡Viva. At ¡Viva Baseball, the contribution of Latin American players to the game is celebrated. You can read about these players in English or Spanish at the Hall of Fame.

W is for "Who's on First?" Baseball's funniest comedy routine is replayed every day at the Hall of Fame. You can continue laughing in this section while you watch Baseball Bloopers.

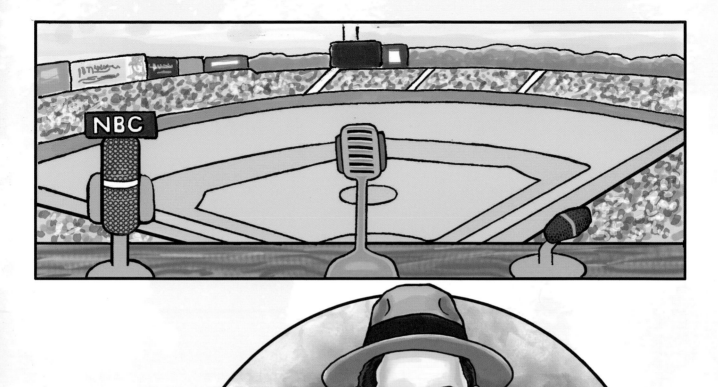

X

is for eXtra. EXtra, eXtra, read all about it! America has had a long-time love affair with baseball. A big reason for this is all of the writers and announcers who have brought baseball to life.

Y is for Yantis. Forest S. Yantis's baseball photographs are on display as you walk through the third floor of the Hall of Fame. Pictures are worth a thousand words.

Z is for Zzz. You will need some sleep after your thrilling day at the Baseball Hall of Fame. Get plenty of rest because you will want to come back another day.

Mary Beth and Mike Young are both teachers in the Athens City School system in Athens, Alabama. Mary Beth is a reading specialist teaching in the Title 1 program and Mike is an American History teacher who also coaches or has coached football, basketball, baseball, and golf at the high school level. They have been married since 1984 and have three wonderful sons, Brian, John Thomas, and Trent. The love of teaching children through academics and sports has been a major part of family life for the Youngs. Their goal is to help students and players find their inner SUPERSTAR.